Little Heroes: Short Inspirational Stories for Children

GEORGE NJOGU

CONTENTS

1 Brave Boy and the Stuck Kitten

Once upon a time, there was a little boy named Timmy. Timmy was a very adventurous boy and loved to explore the great outdoors. He loved climbing trees, playing in the park, and going on long hikes with his family. But there was one thing that Timmy was afraid of - heights. He was terrified of climbing anything higher than his own height and avoided any kind of height-related activities.

One day, as Timmy was playing in his backyard, he heard a faint meowing coming from the trees. He followed the sound and soon discovered that his beloved kitten, Whiskers, was stuck in a tall oak tree. Timmy was devastated and didn't know what to do. He knew that he needed to rescue Whiskers but the thought of climbing that high made him feel sick to his stomach.

But Timmy knew that Whiskers was counting on him, and he couldn't let his fear stop him from saving his beloved kitten. So, he took a deep breath and started climbing the tree. At first, he was shaking and sweating profusely, but as he got closer to Whiskers, he started to feel more confident. He finally reached Whiskers and carefully brought her down to safety.

Timmy was overjoyed that he had saved Whiskers, but he was also proud of himself for facing his fear. He realized that sometimes, we have to face our fears in order to do what's right, and that the rewards of bravery are worth it. From that day on, Timmy's fear of heights slowly started to fade away, and he started to enjoy climbing trees and going on adventures even more.

The experience also taught Timmy the importance of courage and determination. He knew that he couldn't let his fear stop him from doing what was right, and that with a little bit of courage and determination, he could accomplish anything he set his mind to.

From that day on, Timmy grew up to be a confident and brave young man who inspired others to face their fears and do what was right. He was known in the community as a young hero who always put others first and never let fear stop him from helping those in need.

Whiskers, Timmy's kitten, was grateful to Timmy for saving her and never left Timmy's side. They went on many adventures together, and Timmy always remembered the day that he saved Whiskers, and how it helped him to overcome his fear of heights and become a true hero.

2 Community Garden for Feeding Homeless Animals.

Once upon a time, there was a young girl named Maria who was filled with curiosity and ambition. She was always eager to learn new things and explore the world around her. She had a big heart and was always willing to help others and make a positive impact in her community. One day, while playing in her backyard, Maria noticed that the stream that ran behind her house was dirty and filled with litter. She felt sad and disappointed that such a beautiful part of nature was being neglected and mistreated

Maria knew she had to do something about it, she couldn't just stand by and watch the stream get destroyed. She did some research and learned about the importance of clean water and how pollution affects the environment and the animals that lived in it. She also learned about the different ways to clean up and protect the environment.

Determined to make a change, Maria rallied her friends and family and together they organized a community cleanup of the stream. They spread the word, and soon, many of her neighbors joined in on the effort. They worked together to remove trash, plant trees, and install barriers to prevent future pollution.

Their hard work paid off, the stream was now clean, and the wildlife was returning. Fish could be seen swimming in the stream, and birds were singing in the trees. Maria's community was proud of what they had accomplished, and the stream became a popular spot for the community to gather and enjoy nature.

Maria's actions inspired her community to take care of the environment and make a difference in their own neighborhoods. They began to organize regular cleanups, and they also started to educate others about the importance of preserving the environment.

Maria's efforts did not go unnoticed, her community cleanup project was recognized by the local authorities, and she received an award for her outstanding community service. Maria's actions not only improved her neighborhood but also set an example for others to follow.

Maria's community cleanup project taught her about the power of taking action, and the importance of protecting the environment for future generations. She learned that one person can make a difference, and that together, a community can accomplish great things.

From that day on, Maria continued to be an advocate for the environment, and she continued to inspire others to make a difference in their own communities.

3 Friendly Park Cleanup Crew.

Once upon a time, there was a group of friends named Sarah, Michael, and Alex. They lived in a small town and loved to spend their free time at the local park. The park was a beautiful place filled with lush green trees, a pond, and a playground. However, over time, the park had become rundown and dirty. The playground equipment was rusty and the pond was filled with debris. It was no longer a safe place for the community to enjoy.

One day, while they were at the park, the friends noticed how dirty and unsafe the park had become. They knew that something needed to be done to make the park a safe place for everyone to enjoy. They decided to take action and organize a community cleanup of the park.

Sarah, Michael, and Alex rallied their friends and family and together they formed a group to clean up the park. They spread the word and soon, many of their classmates and neighbors joined in on the effort. They worked together to remove trash, repair the playground equipment, and clean up the pond.

Their hard work paid off, the park was now clean and safe for everyone to enjoy. The playground equipment was in good condition, and the pond was clear and clean. Wildlife began to return to the park, and the friends could see birds and fish swimming in the pond.

The community was proud of what they had accomplished, and the park became a popular spot for families to gather and enjoy nature.

The friends' actions inspired the community to take care of the park and make a difference in their own neighborhood. They began to organize regular cleanups, and they also started to educate others about the importance of preserving the environment.

Their efforts did not go unnoticed, the local authorities recognized their work and they were awarded for their community service. The friends' actions not only improved their neighborhood but also set an example for others to follow.

The friends' community cleanup project taught them about the power of teamwork and the importance of taking action to make a positive change. They learned that together, they could accomplish great things and make a real difference in their community. From that day on, they continued to be advocates for their community and inspire others to do the same.

4 Standing Up to Bullies and Making Friends.

Once upon a time, there was a boy named Tim. Tim was a kind and caring child who had a big heart. He always stood up for what was right and was never afraid to speak his mind. He was a leader among his classmates and was well-respected by his teachers and peers.

One day, a new student named David, transferred to Tim's school. David was shy and timid, and he had a hard time fitting in. He was often the target of bullies and was picked on for being different. Tim noticed David's struggles and knew he had to do something to help.

Tim made it a point to talk to David and make him feel welcome at school. He invited him to join him and his friends at lunch and included him in their group activities. Tim also made sure to stand up for David when he was bullied. He would speak out against the bullies and defend David, making sure that they knew that their behavior was not acceptable.

David's confidence began to grow, and he began to make friends and feel more comfortable at school. Tim's kindness and compassion had a positive impact on David's life and helped him to feel included and valued.

Tim's actions did not go unnoticed, his classmates and teachers were inspired by his actions and they too began to reach out to David and make him feel welcome. The school became a more inclusive and supportive community.

Tim's actions taught him about the power of kindness and the importance of standing up for what is right. He learned that small actions can make a big difference and that everyone deserves to be treated with respect and kindness. From that day on, Tim continued to be an advocate for kindness and inclusion, and he inspired others to do the same.

David was grateful for Tim's friendship, he felt like he belonged and he had a sense of purpose in school. Tim's actions not only helped David but also helped the whole school to become a more inclusive and kinder community.

5 Girl's Crafty Mission: Fundraising for Children's Hospital.

Once upon a time, there was a young girl named Emily. Emily was a creative and crafty child who loved to make things. She would spend hours in her room, creating homemade crafts and experimenting with different materials. She was passionate about her hobby and was always looking for ways to improve her skills.

One day, Emily was watching the news and saw a story about a local children's hospital. The hospital was in need of funds to purchase new equipment and provide care for the children who were being treated there. Emily knew she could not stand idly by and had to take action to assist in the situation.

Emily decided to use her craft-making skills to raise money for the children's hospital. She began to create homemade crafts and sell them to her friends and family. She made everything from jewelry to candles, and even homemade soaps. Her creations were a huge hit and soon, she was getting orders from people all over the community.

Emily's hard work paid off, she was able to raise a significant amount of money for the children's hospital. The hospital was able to purchase new equipment and provide better care for the children who were being treated there.

Emily's actions did not go unnoticed, her community was inspired by her kindness and generosity. Many people started to make donations to the children's hospital and others began to volunteer their time. The children's hospital became a community effort, and everyone was working together to make a difference.

Emily's actions taught her about the power of kindness and the importance of giving back to her community. She learned that even small actions can make a big difference and that by working together, they can achieve great things. From that day on, Emily continued to be an advocate for children's hospitals and inspire others to do the same.

The hospital staff was very grateful for Emily's efforts, they saw that her actions had a direct impact on the children they were taking care of. They acknowledged her contributions and gave her a tour of the hospital. She was able to see firsthand how her actions had made a difference in the lives of the children and their families.

6 Kind Boy, Helping Hand.

Once upon a time, there was a young boy named Alex. Alex was a curious and adventurous child who loved to explore his neighborhood. He would often spend his afternoons riding his bike around the streets, taking in all the sights and sounds of his community.

One day, Alex was out on his bike and saw something that caught his attention. An elderly neighbor, Mrs. Thompson, was struggling to carry her groceries back to her house. Her bags were heavy and she was having a hard time keeping her balance. Alex knew he had to help.

Alex rode over to Mrs. Thompson and offered to carry her groceries for her. She gratefully accepted and together they walked back to her house. As they walked, Alex learned that Mrs. Thompson was a widow who lived alone and that she had trouble getting around.

From that day on, Alex made it a point to help Mrs. Thompson with her groceries every week. He would ride his bike over to her house, and help her carry her bags back home. As they spent more time together, Alex learned more about Mrs. Thompson and her life. He learned about her husband who had passed away, her children who lived far away, and the struggles she faced living alone.

Alex's actions made a big difference in Mrs. Thompson's life. She had someone to talk to and someone to help her with her groceries. Alex's kindness and compassion made her feel less alone and more connected to her community.

As Alex helped Mrs. Thompson, he learned about the importance of helping others. He learned that small actions can make a big difference and that by reaching out to others and offering a helping hand, they can make a real impact in someone's life. From that day on, Alex continued to be a helper in his community and inspire others to do the same.

Mrs. Thompson was grateful for Alex's help, she felt like she had a companion, a young friend who cared about her well-being. She felt more confident and safe in her neighborhood, knowing that there was someone who cared about her.

As the weeks passed, Alex and Mrs. Thompson became friends, they would talk and share stories, and she would tell him about her life and the history of their neighborhood. Alex learned a lot from her and he felt like he had a mentor.

7 Girl's Book Club: Uniting The Community

Once upon a time, there was a girl named Sarah. Sarah loved reading and spent most of her time with a book in her hand. She had a big library at her home and would spend hours reading different books. She loved how reading took her to different worlds and how it made her feel.

One day, Sarah saw that not everyone in her neighborhood was as lucky as her. She saw that many kids her age struggled with reading and writing, and they didn't have access to as many books. So, Sarah came up with an idea. She decided to start a book club to promote literacy and bring kids in the neighborhood together.

Sarah invited all the kids in her neighborhood to join the book club. They met every week at the local library and discussed the books they had read. Sarah and her friends would lead the meetings, and everyone would have the chance to share their thoughts and opinions on the book.

As the meetings continued, Sarah saw the impact of her book club. Kids who had struggled with reading were now more confident and enjoying reading more. They were also making new friends and connections within the community. Sarah's book club was not only promoting literacy but also helping kids to explore new books and authors.

Sarah's book club became a big success in the neighborhood, and more and more kids joined. They would select new books to read every month and the meetings were always full of excitement and fun. Sarah's idea had grown into something much bigger than she had ever imagined and she was proud of the positive impact it was having on her community.

8 Overcoming Stuttering: A Boy's Journey to Advocacy.

Once upon a time, there lived a young boy named Timmy. Timmy had always struggled with a stuttering problem, which made it difficult for him to speak in public or even with his classmates. He was often teased and bullied because of his speech impediment, and he felt very self-conscious about it.

Timmy's parents took him to see a speech therapist, and with her help, he began to work on his stuttering. He practiced different exercises and techniques to control his speech and improve his fluency. It was a long and challenging journey, but Timmy was determined to overcome his stuttering.

As Timmy's speech improved, he began to gain confidence in himself. He started to speak up more in class and even joined the school debate team. Timmy found that he had a talent for public speaking and he enjoyed being in front of an audience.

Timmy's hard work paid off when he won a school-wide public speaking competition. He was thrilled to have overcome his stuttering and to have achieved something he never thought possible.

Timmy's success inspired him to become an advocate for other children with speech difficulties. He began to speak at schools and events about his own journey and the importance of seeking help if you have a speech impediment. He also shared tips and techniques that helped him with his own stuttering.

Timmy's speeches were well received and he became a role model for many children. He showed them that with hard work and determination, they could also overcome their speech difficulties.

As Timmy grew older, he continued to speak in public and advocate for children with speech difficulties. He became an accomplished public speaker and even wrote a book about his experiences, which helped many people.

Timmy's story teaches us that with hard work and determination, we can overcome any obstacle and achieve our goals. It's also a reminder that everyone has their own challenges to face, and that we should be kind and supportive of one another.

As Timmy continued to speak at events, he also began to work with speech therapists and educators to develop new techniques and strategies to help children with speech difficulties. He became a respected authority on the topic and his insights helped many children and their families.

In addition to his public speaking, Timmy also started a support group for children with speech difficulties. He provided a safe and supportive space for children to share their experiences and offer each other encouragement and advice. The group quickly grew in popularity and helped many children feel less alone in their struggles.

Timmy's dedication to helping children with speech difficulties did not go unnoticed. He was honored with several awards for his advocacy and community service. He also received recognition from organizations that support people with speech difficulties.

Despite all of his accomplishments, Timmy never forgot the struggles he faced as a child. He always remained humble and grateful for the help he received along the way. He said that he wanted to give back to the community, and he did so by helping others who were going through the same struggles he went through.

In the end, Timmy's journey taught us that no matter what challenges we face, we have the power to overcome them. It also showed us that everyone has the potential to make a positive impact on the world and to help others.

Timmy is a true inspiration and a shining example of what one person can accomplish when they set their mind to it.

9 Honesty Lesson: A Boy's Mistake.

Long ago, there existed a young boy by the name of Max. He was a curious and adventurous child, always eager to explore the world around him. One day, while playing with his friends at the park, they came across a shiny toy car. It looked brand new and was just lying there as if it had been abandoned. Without thinking, they picked it up and started playing with it, having the time of their lives.

As the day went on, Max started to feel uneasy about the toy car. He realized that it must have belonged to someone and that they would be missing it. He knew he had to do the right thing and return the toy car to its rightful owner. He tried to find out who that was, but it proved to be a difficult task, as no one seemed to know anything about it.

Days went by and Max couldn't shake off the feeling of guilt. He knew he had to come clean and tell the truth. He went to his teacher and confessed what he and his friends had done. His teacher listened carefully and praised him for his honesty. She told him that it was the right thing to do, and that he should never be afraid to admit when he's made a mistake.

Max felt a weight lifted off his shoulders. He knew he had to find the toy car's owner and return it to them. He went back to the park and asked around, but no one seemed to know anything. He even went to the nearby stores and asked if anyone had reported a lost toy car, but to no avail. Max was determined not to give up, he knew he had to do this for his own peace of mind.

One day, while Max was walking home from school, he saw an elderly man sitting on a bench in the park. The man looked sad and forlorn, and Max felt a pang of recognition. The toy car belonged to him! The old man told Max that he had lost the toy car a few weeks ago and had been looking for it ever since. It was his favorite toy and he had many fond memories associated with it.

Max was overjoyed that he had finally found the toy car's owner. He apologized for taking it and explained that he and his friends had found it and played with it, but that he now realized it wasn't theirs to take. The old man was incredibly grateful and thanked Max for his honesty and kindness. He even invited Max to come and play with the toy car anytime he wanted.

Max learned an important lesson that day. Being truthful is always the right choice, even if it may be challenging. He was proud of himself for doing the right thing and for making an old man's day. He also started a "Honesty Club" at school, to teach other kids the importance of being truthful, even when it's tough. From then on

Max made sure to always be honest and to take responsibility for his actions. He knew that it was the only way to truly be at peace with himself. He also made sure to spread the message of honesty to his friends and classmates, encouraging them to do the same.

The "Honesty Club" quickly grew in popularity, with more and more students joining every day. They would meet weekly and talk about ways to practice honesty in their everyday lives. They even organized a "Honesty Day" at school where they would share their own stories and encourage others to be truthful.

Max's honesty and kindness had a ripple effect throughout the community. People started to notice the change in him and were inspired to do the same. His actions had a positive impact on those around him and helped create a more trustworthy and honest community.

Max learned that by being honest and taking responsibility for his actions, he could make a real difference in the world. He knew that it was the little things that made the biggest impact and that by being true to himself, he could be a role model for others to follow.

From that day on, Max was known as the "Honest Boy", a shining example of what it means to be true to oneself and to others. And that toy car will always be a reminder of the lesson he learned, the power of honesty and the importance of taking responsibility for one's actions.

10 Girl's Community Clean-Up Adventure

Once upon a time, there was a young girl named Jenna. Jenna loved her community and spent a lot of time playing outside with her friends. She loved the local park, where they would play tag, swing on the swings and have picnics. But one day, while Jenna was playing at the park, she noticed something that made her very upset. The park was dirty and cluttered with litter. Jenna saw broken bottles, candy wrappers and plastic bags everywhere. She realized that if she and her friends didn't take care of the park, no one else would.

Jenna knew she had to do something to help. She gathered her friends together and explained to them what she had noticed. They all agreed that the park was in bad shape and that they needed to take action. Jenna came up with a plan to clean up the park, and her friends were more than happy to help. They decided to start a community clean-up program.

The first thing Jenna and her friends did was to put up flyers all around the community, inviting people to join the community clean-up program. They also went door to door, talking to people and explaining to them the importance of taking care of the park. They were surprised by how many people were willing to help.

The day of the clean-up arrived, and Jenna was excited to see so many people turn up. There were kids, adults, and even some older people, all ready to help. They worked together to pick up litter, sweep the paths, and clean the playground equipment. It was hard work, but everyone was having a good time.

After several hours of hard work, the park was finally clean. Jenna and her friends had done it. The park was now a safe and beautiful place for everyone to enjoy. Jenna felt proud of what they had achieved and realized that by working together, they could make a real difference in the community.

From that day on, Jenna and her friends organized regular clean-up days at the park. They also started a recycling program, where they collected plastic bottles and cans, and took them to the recycling center. They even planted some flowers and trees, making the park even more beautiful.

Jenna learned an important lesson that day. She learned that by taking care of our shared spaces, we can make the world a better place. She also learned that small actions can lead to big changes, and that by working together, we can accomplish great things.

Years went by, and Jenna grew up, but she never forgot the lessons she had learned. She continued to be an active member of her community, always looking for ways to make it a better place. She was a role model for many young people, inspiring them to take action and make a difference in their own communities.

Jenna's community clean-up program was a great success, and it was still going strong years later. The park was now a place where people from all over the community came to enjoy, and it was all thanks to Jenna and her friends who took the initiative to make a difference. They had proved that anyone, no matter their age, can make a positive impact on their community.

10 Inclusion and Kindness: A Boy's Journey

Once upon a time, there was a boy named Jack who attended a small elementary school in a quiet town. Jack was a kind and empathetic boy, who always went out of his way to help others. One day, a new student named Timmy joined his class. Timmy was a little different from the other students. He had special needs and struggled to communicate and participate in class activities.

At first, the other students didn't know how to interact with Timmy, and he often felt left out. Jack, however, saw the potential in Timmy and decided to take action. He began to spend time with Timmy during recess and lunch, trying to understand his needs and interests. Jack soon realized that Timmy had a love for art and music.

With this new understanding, Jack came up with a plan to include Timmy in school activities. He convinced the art teacher to let Timmy help with creating decorations for the school's upcoming art fair. Jack also helped Timmy practice playing a simple song on the piano during music class.

Timmy's classmates were amazed at how much he had improved and how much he was able to contribute to the school's art fair. They had never seen him so happy and engaged before. Timmy's art and music creations were a hit at the fair, and he even won first place in the art category.

The other students began to see Timmy in a new light and they started to include him in their activities. They realized that he had a lot to offer and that he was just like them. Timmy's confidence grew, and he began to participate more in class and make new friends.

Jack's efforts to include Timmy in school activities not only helped Timmy but also brought the class closer together. They learned that everyone is unique and special in their own way, and that by being kind and empathetic, they could make a positive impact on someone's life.

As Timmy's confidence grew, so did his love for art and music. He continued to excel in these areas and even began to participate in community events, showcasing his talents. Timmy's classmates were proud of him and they all cheered him on.

Years went by, and Jack and Timmy graduated from elementary school. They remained friends and continued to support each other in their endeavors. Jack's actions had not only made a positive impact on Timmy's life but also on the lives of many other students who were also struggling to find acceptance and inclusion.

In high school, Timmy continued to excel in art and music, and even went on to attend a prestigious art school after graduation. Jack went on to study engineering, but he always made time to visit Timmy and attend his art shows. They remained close friends throughout their lives, and Timmy always credited Jack with helping him to find his place in the world.

Years later, when Jack and Timmy were adults, they both returned to their hometown to give back to the community that had helped shape them into the men they had become. Jack became a mentor for young students, helping them to find their passions and overcome any obstacles they may be facing. Timmy became an art teacher at the elementary school, where he shared his love for art with the next generation of students.

Together, Jack and Timmy continued to inspire the students and teachers at the school, showing them that kindness and empathy can change lives. They were a shining example of how one small act of kindness can make a world of difference. They proved that inclusion and acceptance is key for everyone to thrive and succeed in life.